*To Melissa, Mari, and her mother
who made it work—wonderfully.*

Why Can't You Stay Home With Me?

A Book About Working Mothers

By Barbara Shook Hazen
Illustrated by Deborah Borgo

*Prepared with the cooperation of Bernice Berk, Ph.D.,
of the Bank Street College of Education*

A GOLDEN BOOK · NEW YORK

Western Publishing Company, Inc., Racine, Wisconsin 53404

Note to Parents

As more and more women go into the work force, more and more children are dealing with having their mothers away from home during the day. Some children are resentful, and some are not. But the task for the mother is often formidable. She must try to be all things for all people. She has to try to do her job thoroughly and well, she must still take care of her house, and she must give her children the time and attention they need. It isn't always easy.

Not only can fathers pitch in and do dishes, but children can rise to the occasion as well. It's a wonderful role model for children to see their mothers working. It also shows children that everyone has responsibilities and obligations which must be met. Children really like the feeling of being needed and participating members of their families. They can accept the responsibility of having certain jobs that should be done to help Mommy. Instead of asking your children to leave you alone and watch TV while you do all the chores, you can ask them to help. With both younger and older children, it's more fun to work along with them. Anything—from putting the clothes in the washing machine, to separating the white things from the colored things, to setting the table or mixing the salad dressing—is fun, as long as you do it together. It gives you both a chance to talk and share the day's activities instead of screaming and yelling at them all the time. When your children are through helping you with your chores, you can help them with theirs—homework, tidying up their rooms, etc.

It's also nice to set aside a small block of time each day when you can talk quietly and uninterruptedly with your children. Perhaps before bed is best for some. You can also try cutting down a little on TV watching. That would give you all an island of quiet in which to share thoughts and experiences, and let your children know you're still interested in them and care for them.

Not only does having the whole family share the workload, share their feelings, and share the day's events open the lines of communication, it allows both parents to feel they're not missing as much of their children's growth and progress to adulthood.

—The Editors

Melissa's mother works, which means mornings are
sometimes hectic.

Everyone hurries. Everyone has to help. Everyone
is busy.

Melissa has to hunt for her homework herself, and make her bed, and braid her hair the best she can.

Melissa's mother walks Melissa to school, which is on her way to work. It's a special time when they can talk about all sorts of things.

Just outside the school door, Melissa's mother hugs her hard and says, "Have a good day. I love you, and I'll miss you a bundle."

Melissa hates to see her mother go. But during school she is too busy to miss her very much.

Melissa's mother works, which means she can't pick
Melissa up after school. That's when Melissa misses her
mother the most.

Different people pick Melissa up—sometimes Gram,
sometimes Mrs. Maxwell next door, and sometimes
Billy's mother.

Once in a while, Melissa's father picks her up when
he is home early from a business trip.

Sometimes Melissa misses her mother because it's hard to sit down and do her homework when her mother isn't around, and it's hard to have to wait until "later" to tell her something.

But most of the time Melissa has fun doing different
things with the different people who take care of her.
Sometimes they even let her do things her mother
won't, like watch TV before her homework is done, or
eat ice cream in the middle of the afternoon.

Three days a week Melissa goes to Mrs. Sethness' Day Center. There she plays with other children her age, and learns new things to do.

Mrs. Sethness is nice, but she doesn't know certain things about Melissa the way her mother does. She doesn't know Melissa likes baseball better than paints, and chocolate better than vanilla.

So Melissa tells her, and tries new things and learns to like them, too.

Melissa's mother works, so she can't *always* be with Melissa on special occasions, no matter how much she wants to and tries.

She missed Field Day, when Melissa hit her first home run…

...and the school play, when Melissa was Captain Cook. Melissa was especially sorry her mother couldn't make that, but she was glad her cousins could.

Melissa's mother works, so she can't always stay home
when Melissa wants her to, like during school vacations.

One day Melissa said, "Please don't go. I want *you* to
stay home with me."

"That sounds nice," said Melissa's mother. "But I have
to think of my job."

"You like your dumb old job more than me," Melissa said.

"I love you a zillion times more than any job," her mother said. "Always remember that. Now have a nice day with Mrs. Maxwell, and I'll call you later."

By the time her mother called, Melissa was having a
nice time making a pot holder.

By the time her mother got home, Melissa had it
finished. She gave it to her mother and said, "Surprise!"

"What a nice surprise!" her mother said. "I didn't
know you knew how to weave."

"I didn't—but I do now," said Melissa, giving Mrs.
Maxwell and her mother both hugs.

Because Melissa's mother works, she can't always be there when Melissa wants her. But she is there zip-quick when Melissa really needs her, and always will be.

"Like the time I was hit in the head with the baseball," Melissa recalls one day when she and her mother are talking and feeding the birds.

Melissa remembers her mother rushing to school in a big, yellow taxi—and comforting her.

Because Melissa's mother works, now there is enough money to eat out more,

and get Melissa a great new school coat, and go to a woodsy cabin on a nice vacation.

Her mother's job started Melissa thinking about the kind of work she might like to do someday when she grows up.

Some days she thinks she might like to work in an office the way her mother does...or travel and sell things like her father.

Other days she thinks she might like to be a taxi driver, or a doctor, or start a Melissa Day-Care Center on the moon.

She thinks about the work her friends' mothers do, and looks at books about interesting jobs.

One very special day Melissa visits her mother's office, when she has a holiday and her mother doesn't.

Melissa sits in her mother's big desk chair, and touches her mother's things very carefully.

It pleases her to see a picture of herself on her mother's desk.

"You see, Pumpkin, I miss you a lot when I'm not with you," her mother says, as they share a talk and good jelly doughnuts from the wagon.

"Sometimes I hate it when I want you home and you're at work," Melissa tells her mother. "And sometimes I hate it when you come home tired and grumpy."

"Some days are like that," says Melissa's mother. "But my being tired and grumpy doesn't mean I'm angry with you. And you're getting better at waiting until I get over my grumpiness. Sometimes you do nice things for me. I like that."

"But most days I don't mind," said Melissa, drawing a big smile face on her mother's memo pad. "Because I can do more things by myself now. When I help you, that makes me feel grown-up."

"Which makes me very happy and very proud of you,"
says Melissa's mother.

"That makes the time we're together even better,"
adds Melissa.